Who Made This Big Mess?

Written by **Andrew Gutelle**

Illustrated by **Sally Schaedler**

TIME LIFE Kids™

ALEXANDRIA,
VIRGINIA

Loonette and her doll Molly loved the Big Comfy Couch. It was anything they wanted it to be—a spaceship, a castle, or even the bumpy back of a camel.

"I'm hot," said Loonette after their long, bouncy camel ride. "What can we play to cool off?"

"I know!" shouted Loonette.
"We can have a beach party!"
Loonette looked for all
the things she and
Molly needed.

She found her
beach hat....

And her flippy-floppy
beach slippers....

And Molly's
pail and shovel....

But she could not find her beachball anywhere!

"My beachball must be here somewhere," insisted Loonette. "Come on, Molly. Let's find it!"

First Loonette looked underneath the Big Comfy Couch. Fuzzy and Wuzzy, the two dustbunnies, scampered away. Loonette did not see them, but she did find her tennis racket and a crazy collection of clown shoes.

Loonette scooped up the shoes and
laid them one by one across the room.
Then she held her
tennis racket like a
magnifying glass.
She pretended she
was Detective
Loonette.

"Aha!" said the detective. "These footprints may lead to the missing ball!"

The trail of silly shoes did not lead to the beachball. Instead it ended at Loonette's toy shelves. They were jammed and crammed with her favorite things.

"Maybe my beachball is here," she said.

Loonette peeked and poked inside the boxes and bins. Then on the tippy-top shelf she spied an old cardboard box. "My tea set!" she said happily.

Loonette and Molly stopped
looking for the beachball just long
enough to have a tea party. All
their guests had a delightful time.

After the party, the search continued. "Did my beach-ball roll under my vanity?" wondered Loonette. She bent down to look. There was no ball, but there was a rumpled, crumpled pile of dress-up clothes.

In the pile Loonette found a long black cape, a funny mustache, and a tall top hat. She became the Incredible Loonini, the world's trickiest magician. When she pulled a rabbit out of her hat, everyone was amazed!

Loonette's room was now so
messy that she could not walk across it. Instead
she jumped up on the Big Comfy Couch to look
for her beachball. Reaching deep into the
cushions, she pulled out her glasses.

Loonette read to Molly. She read books about
dragons, snowflakes, ballerinas, and baseball.

When Loonette finished reading, she looked around the room. Not only was her beachball still missing, there was so much clutter that she could not find or do anything!

"WHO made this BIG MESS?" she asked.

Molly didn't say a word.

"Me? Oh right, I guess I did," Loonette admitted. "Well then, I'd better clean it up! It's only fair. So get ready for the Ten Second Tidy. Ready. Set. Go...."

Like an acrobat,
Loonette leaped into
action. She dashed this
way and that....

Packing....

Stacking....

Fluffing....

And Stuffing....

When Loonette finished, the room was neater than Granny Garbanzo's garden. That's when she noticed something in the corner next to Molly.

"My beachball!" she cried. "That's what I like best about tidying up, Molly. Sometimes you find the thing you want the most!"

Just in time for the
best beach party ever!